A Bride for McKenzie

Book One

The Sheriff's Mail Order Bride

Cheryl Wright

A Bride for McKenzie

(The Sheriff's Mail Order Bride – Book One)

Copyright ©2021 by Cheryl Wright

Cover Artist: Black Widow Books

Editing: Amber Downey

Dedication

To Margaret Tanner, my very dear friend and fellow author, for her enduring encouragement and friendship.

To Alan, my husband of over forty-six years, who has been a relentless supporter of my writing and dreams for many years.

To Virginia McKevitt, my cover artist and friend, who always creates the most amazing covers for my books, thank you.

To You, my wonderful readers, who encourage me to continue writing these stories. It is such a joy knowing so many of you enjoy reading my stories as much as I love writing them for you.

Table of Contents

Chapter One

Ontario, Canada – 1880's

Verity LeFebvre gaped open-mouthed at her uncle. "You can't do that," she said far more calmly than she felt. "Father said I had a home here forever."

Louis LeFebvre sneered. "Well, he's not here, and I say no. I want the place to myself and my new bride. What you want doesn't factor into it."

"But this is my home!"

Her uncle sneered. "Not anymore, it's not. I inherited everything. Nothing here is yours, including those expensive gowns your father indulged in for you." He rubbed his hands together. "They will fit my new bride perfectly. And the jewelry that belongs to me. There is nothing in this house that belongs to you." His laugh came out more like a cackle, and the sound cut through her.

Verity didn't remember her uncle. According to her father, he'd always had a wanderlust, and traveled all around Canada spreading the word of God. Father had always made him sound like such a wonderful man, and had even supported him with a generous monthly allowance for all those years. However, his actions now proved he was far from wonderful or a God-fearing man, which totally confused her.

It wasn't that she particularly wanted any of those things, but they were all she had left of her mother. She'd inherited the jewelry, and it had been presented to her when she came of age. Didn't that mean it was legally hers?

Verity was certain this was not what Father would have wanted. When you were as rich as Pierre LeFebvre, you kept your will up to date. Heck, he'd ensured everything was perfect as she grew up. Nothing was too good for his only child. He had even sent her to finishing school in Switzerland. It had been the best time of her life and also the worst.

She had missed her father immensely, but also all her friends left behind. Verity learned so much more than she could ever learn back here in Canada but was isolated from everyone she knew. By the time she returned home, those who were once close friends were complete strangers – they had changed so much, and some had even married and moved away.

"Pack up your things and get out. You are not wanted here." He sneered again, and his intent rolled off him in waves. The best thing was for Verity to get out as quickly as she possibly could.

Her heart pounded, and she was suddenly light-headed. Verity grabbed the back of the kitchen chair to stop herself from collapsing in front of the fiend. *What would she do now?*

As the owner of the *Ontario Shipping Line*, her father was an extremely wealthy man, and she'd had no need to go out to work or even to cook. She only knew her way around a kitchen because of Marguerite, their cook, but her skills were basic. Very basic. The dear old soul had been with the family for over twenty years, and as it turned out, was a cousin of Pierre's two times removed. Dear kind Marguerite had fallen on hard times, and Verity's father had taken her in. She became his live-in housekeeper and cook, knowing she would never be without a welcoming home to live in.

"You never know what's ahead," Cook had said when she decided to teach Verity the basics of cooking. "I don't trust that uncle of yours, not one little bit." As it turned out, she was right. How two brothers could be so different, Verity would never know.

The thought of Marguerite made her heart hollow. The dear old soul had literally keeled over less than a week ago and died in front of Verity's eyes. There had been nothing anyone could do; she was dead before she hit the floor.

She fought back the tears that threatened to fall at the memory of it all. The last thing she would do was let her revolting uncle see her distress.

Things had changed dramatically for Verity after her father perished in an accident almost a year ago. She was shocked to discover she had not been accommodated in her father's will, although he had told her some years earlier, she would inherit everything should anything happen to him. Of course, neither of them anticipated his untimely death, and according to her uncle, his will wasn't updated in time. It was rather perplexing, as Father had told her repeatedly she inherited everything and that no matter what, she would always have a home in this house – the one she was born in. It was the same one her mother had died in giving her life.

Father had never recovered from his wife's death but had ensured Verity had a good life, nonetheless. Upon Father's death, Uncle Louis had inherited it all and had moved in far too quickly for Verity's liking. Until Marguerite's untimely death, he'd been eerily subdued. Once her last form of defense was gone, his entire personality changed, and now this. The man couldn't wait to rid himself of her.

What she would do now, she had no idea. The only thing she knew for certain was her wretched uncle had given her three days to pack up her things and leave. Where she would go from here was completely beyond her, and for all Verity knew, she could be living on the streets in a matter of days.

Carson's Hollow, Montana

Sheriff McKenzie Dunn paced the boardwalk. It was foolishness. *Utter foolishness*, he muttered to himself as he waited for the stagecoach to arrive. His first mistake was allowing himself to be coerced into writing to a mail order bride agency. His second was accepting a bride without any correspondence.

Not even one letter!

He accepted she was in dire straights but was he making the biggest mistake of his life? McKenzie glanced up as he heard the sound of horses' hooves. Dust filled the air as the stagecoach rounded the corner, and his heart pounded. Within minutes his bride would arrive. He pulled out the telegram he'd been sent and checked the details again.

Verity LeFebvre. It sounded like a highfalutin name that some rich kid might have. *Did that mean his bride would be spoiled? A demanding debutante who thought she was coming to a mansion?* Well, he had news for her. He lived in the small sheriff's house not far out of town. He wasn't rich, far from it, and he sure as heck had no intention of bowing down to any demands she might make.

Darn it, she probably didn't even know how to cook. And wasn't that the reason he'd sent for a bride to begin with? To have decent home-cooked food in his belly? His friend Luke Carson sent for a bride and ended up with a great cook. Not to mention the two were madly in love.

He wanted that too but now regretted his hasty decision. Unfortunately, with his bride literally around the corner, it was far too late for that.

McKenzie groaned as the stagecoach pulled to a halt in front of him. He craned his neck to try and get a glimpse of his bride.

In reality, it wasn't too late to change his mind, but he would never leave a woman in the lurch. He'd promised to marry her, and that was exactly what he would do.

As the passengers began to alight from the coach, McKenzie knew exactly which one was his bride, and all his fears suddenly came to fruition.

McKenzie looked her up and down. Just as he'd feared, she was a rich kid. At least, she came from a wealthy background and was far from a kid. Her clothes had given her away – hers was not an off-the-rack gown that could be found at the mercantile of any town, even a two-horse town like Carson's Hollow. This gown was custom-made, a one-off creation that fitted its owner perfectly; he had absolutely no doubt about it. His eyes shifted to the shiny boots she wore. They appeared to be of the finest leather. Why would someone with this kind of money behind her need to become a mail order bride? And why the urgency?

It was beyond him.

She stepped down from the coach and glanced about. She spotted his sheriff's badge and wore a look of relief. She appeared to be in her late twenties, which was good. He was not into very young women – he preferred someone a little more mature.

"McKenzie Dunn? Sheriff McKenzie Dunn?" Her voice wavered as though she were completely unsure of herself, which surprised McKenzie. At first glance, she appeared confident, totally self-assured. He now knew that wasn't the case.

"Verity?" Of course it was her, otherwise, she wouldn't have known his name. McKenzie could kick himself – he couldn't look more of a fool than he already felt.

"Your luggage, Miss LeFebvre." The stagecoach driver deposited two large trunks on the platform, and McKenzie gaped at them. It appeared more and more this woman, this Verity LeFebvre, did not need his help.

He stepped forward to assist her, and that's when he noticed them - the worried lines around her eyes and the tears shimmering beneath the surface. Her face was etched in pain, not to mention embarrassment. Whatever brought her here had caused deep concern and anxiety. McKenzie had no compulsion to make things worse for her.

"I must look a fright," she said quietly, trying to straighten out the wrinkles on her gown. It was far too late for that. She brushed back the stray hair that was hovering across her eyes, but it was a fruitless exercise. "Is there somewhere I can tidy up?"

"Through there," he said, pointing toward the stagecoach office. The privy was there, and there was a small mirror. She could tidy herself up, at least a little. "I'll take care of your luggage."

She nodded and headed in the direction he'd sent her. McKenzie's heart pounded. What sort of mess had he gotten himself into? He dare not even think.

Verity stood just inside the door of the stagecoach office, feeling far better than she'd entered. A splash of cold water to her face had made all the difference. Not that she'd been able to do much. But removing her bonnet and brushing her hair back with her fingers made her look and feel more like the lady she was brought up to be. When she'd arrived, she not surprisingly was unkempt and fatigued. She felt a little more human now despite her days of travel.

She took a deep breath and let it out slowly. Her prospective husband seemed like a decent man. Well, he was a Sheriff after all. Did he live in a reasonably sized house? She couldn't even begin to imagine what she'd let herself in for. Father's mansion was far too big with its twelve bedrooms, *but please God*, she prayed, let it be more than a rundown one-bedroom shack.

Heating and a decent stove would be good too. If there were at least two fireplaces, she'd be happy. Somewhere she could stand and warm her hands in the cold weather. Verity realized beggars could not be choosers, but some basic necessities would be nice.

A shudder ran through her. This was not the sort of thing she should be asking God to provide. She was being selfish and most definitely un-Christian. Praying was for important things, not materialistic and selfish endeavors. She prayed for forgiveness and stepped outside.

He glanced up as she left the small building and smiled. He'd appeared somewhat uncaring before, and she'd worried he would be a heartless man. Verity imagined that in his line of work, it would be easy to do. But that smile changed everything. It seemed to bring out some of his muted personality. He wasn't a bad looking man either. Quite easy on the eyes, and that helped a lot.

"Feeling better?" He stood by her luggage, as he promised to do.

"Much better, thank you." Her breath came whooshing out, and she felt heat crawl up her face.

He chuckled, then put his hand to his mouth to try and cover his indiscretion, but it was too late. She'd already seen it. She pursed her lips, and he grinned. *Was he really so easygoing?* Perhaps life with the sheriff wouldn't be so bad after all, but she wasn't certain about this tiny town. She glanced about. It certainly was small, not even a quarter of Ontario where she'd come from, but unless McKenzie Dunn reneged on his promise, it was about to become her home.

Pastor Petrie was on standby. McKenzie had arranged for him to marry them as soon as his bride arrived. Better to get it over and done with, he'd decided. He still had reservations about this marriage, but the promise had been made, and he wouldn't back out of it. *Not now, not ever.*

If he'd spoken up when she'd arrived, well, perhaps things might have worked out better. She'd barely said a word to him, and she still seemed rather...standoffish. Perhaps that was her way, but it didn't mean he had to like it.

His arm hooked through his bride's, McKenzie led her toward the small church, the only one in Carson's Hollow. He'd already deposited her trunks on the wagon, and then they'd headed off. Why anyone needed that much luggage, he'd never know. Each trunk was incredibly heavy – it was as though she'd brought absolutely everything she owned.

The thought gave him pause. Perhaps that's exactly what she'd done. "What made it such a rush?" he suddenly blurted out.

She turned and stared at him. "My uncle..." She was unable to finish the sentence and was clearly on the verge of tears, so he didn't push her further. He'd carried out so many interrogations in his time as Sheriff that he knew the look intimately. He wouldn't get anything more out of her now. She was clearly upset, and anything more he asked would make things far worse. Instead, he nodded.

McKenzie stepped forward and opened the intricately carved door to the church, where they found the pastor pottering about in the church, apparently filling in time as he waited for them. "You're sure about this?" he whispered as they headed toward the front of the church.

"I'm sure." She didn't sound positive, and it worried him, but he wasn't forcing her, and that was all that mattered.

"McKenzie!" Pastor Petrie said joyfully as he rubbed his hands together. "And who might this lovely lady be?"

"Pastor Petrie, let me introduce you to my bride, Verity LeFebvre."

"Very pleased to meet you, my dear. Now, I must ask, are you going into this marriage of your own volition?"

She nodded, then stared at him as though shocked at the question. "Absolutely," she said quietly, her voice wavering again. "No one is forcing me."

McKenzie was still convinced there was more to it, but she'd made her choice.

It wasn't long, and they had been pronounced man and wife. When the pastor told him he could kiss his bride, he brushed his lips lightly across hers, and it sent a shudder coursing through him. It could only get better than this, he thought as he stared into her sad brown eyes.

"This is it. Home," McKenzie said as he climbed down off the wagon. Ordinarily, he would not have taken a wagon such a short distance – after all, it was an easy walk from the stage office to his home. Knowing, or at least assuming, his bride would have luggage, he hired a horse and wagon from the livery. It seemed rather silly at the time, but now he was pleased he'd made the effort.

She was rather petite, compared to his large size, but pretty. Beautiful, in fact. His hands held tight to her waist as he slowly brought her down from the wagon. He gazed into her eyes and felt as though he could get lost in her soul. Sadly, his bride did not seem as elated to be married to him as McKenzie had hoped. She glanced over his shoulder at the cottage they would live in as husband and wife. The look of disdain on her face was not lost on him.

He put her gently to the ground and stared down into her face. "What do you think?" He watched as she swallowed hard. It was probably the most honest answer he would get.

"It looks...homely." For the first time, McKenzie noticed the slight French accent to her words.

It was apparent the cottage was far smaller than she was used to, but there was nothing to be done about it. This was their home, and that was the end of it. He turned and unlocked the door, swinging it open. Then he scooped his bride up and carried her across the threshold. Their faces were close, closer than they'd been before, except for that poor excuse of a kiss they'd had in the church.

He watched as her eyes fluttered closed, then opened again to stare at him. Her arms slipped up around his neck, then she suddenly pulled away again. More than anything, he wanted to kiss her again, but it wasn't his choice to make. She might be his wife, but Verity was a complete stranger. There were two things he knew about her; she came a very long way to marry him. The other was peculiar – she appeared rich but desperately needed to become a mail order bride.

Absolutely none of it made sense.

He gently put her to the floor, then slammed the door closed behind him. She flinched at the noise, and he regretted being so energetic about it. "Sorry," he said quietly. "I didn't mean to startle you."

She glanced up at him. "I wasn't expecting it, that's all." She smiled, but McKenzie could see her smile was fake. She was putting on a show for him, and it was the last thing he wanted from his new wife.

He watched as she glanced about. She didn't seem particularly happy but didn't voice her concerns as she strolled into the kitchen and looked over the stove. "You can cook, right?" he asked, concern clouding his thoughts.

She glanced up at him. "Enough to make sure you don't go hungry." She smiled, and this time, it was a genuine reaction, not one she'd forced. "Where's the pantry?"

He stared down at the ground, embarrassed to admit the truth. "It's through there," he said, pointing, but she was gone before he could finish the sentence. "There's nothing in there except a loaf of bread and some butter," he finished as he rounded the corner.

The shocked look on her face told him they needed to go shopping. But tonight, he would take his bride to the diner to celebrate.

The trunks were heavy – McKenzie couldn't believe how weighty they were. "What do you have in here, rocks?" He chuckled, but Verity didn't share his mirth.

"I brought my favorite books with me, along with my mother's prized crockery. That foul…" She took a deep breath and let it out slowly. "My uncle would not appreciate them. Besides, the crockery was given to me after my mother passed. A dowry of sorts."

He nodded but knew there was far more to her story than Verity had let on. "The second one is not as heavy." It was a statement, not really a question. "I'll put them in the spare room. That way, you can unpack whenever you are ready."

She nodded, and tension took over her expression. "That one has my clothes, the jewelry left to me by my mother, as well as those given to me as gifts."

For some reason, she suddenly seemed terribly upset and on the verge of tears. He moved closer to her. "Tell me what's going on? Maybe I can help."

He pulled her close and caressed her back, but she suddenly pulled away. "My uncle inherited everything when my father died. He said I couldn't take the jewelry, that it was part of his inheritance. Since I inherited most of it when Mother passed on, and received the rest as gifts, surely they belong to me?"

She searched his face for answers. "I would have thought so." He scratched his head. "I'm almost certain that would be the case, but we can consult with the town solicitor and double-check."

The relief on her face was palpable. "I'm not a thief. I only took what I believed was mine. Uncle told me I had to leave my clothes behind too, but since they were gifts from my father, I took those as well." She lifted her chin as if in defiance, and a shudder ran through him. McKenzie had married himself a feisty woman, and he wondered what life with her would be like.

One thing he did know, this uncle must be a lowdown skunk to try and deprive his niece of items that were rightly hers. It made him wonder if the will was legitimate or whether he'd intentionally deprived Verity of her inheritance through illegal means. It was worth looking into.

"I'll probably never wear any of those gowns or that fancy jewelry again, but that's beside the point," she said quietly. "Most of the jewelry belonged to my mother, and it's all I have left of her besides the crockery. And that could be gone in a flash if the trunk was dropped." She sighed heavily. "For all I know, it could have been ruined on the trip here."

His heart broke for this woman he barely knew; she had been handed a raw deal. At least now he knew why she was desperate to become a mail order bride.

McKenzie pulled her close again and enveloped her in his warmth. This time she didn't pull away.

Chapter Two

"The food here is delicious." McKenzie watched as his bride devoured her meal. "Our cook back home was a wonderful cook. I didn't think anyone could cook better than her."

"Jeannie, the owner of the diner, is a terrific cook. I come here every night for supper." She frowned at him. "At least I did. I'm hoping for more home-cooked meals now."

Verity put down her knife and fork. "You don't expect me to cook this well, I hope. Marguerite taught me some things, but I don't know if it's enough to satisfy your belly." McKenzie stared at her as she spoke. He knew he shouldn't, but apart from her overwhelming beauty, her slight accent was intriguing.

"I'm sure we will work something out." He reached across and held her hand. "Heck, if we have to come here to eat every night, so be it. I'm certain Jeannie won't mind." He winked at his bride, and she blushed. The color creeping up her face was cute, but she probably didn't think so. She suddenly snatched her hand out of his grip and plied her hands to her cheeks. It made him chuckle.

"What is so funny?" she demanded, frowning at him.

He raised his eyebrows in question. "You look…delightful when you blush."

She huffed in protest, then lifted her cutlery again, intent on ignoring his comment. Then she glanced up and screwed up her cute little nose. She smiled coyly, then went back to eating her meal. His wife was such a sweet thing, and despite her age, seemed rather naïve and unworldly.

Not that he was worldly because he wasn't, but coming from a wealthy background, he thought she would be well traveled and know far more than a genteel lady should. But who was he to know these things? Suddenly he wanted to know everything there was to know about his bride but also didn't want to bombard her with questions.

Nice and slow; that's how he had to play this. His enthusiasm would be his undoing if he wasn't careful. Isn't that how he did his job? With patience and understanding where needed? He had the skills, so McKenzie now had to ensure he did the same thing with Verity.

She glanced up at him with a perplexed look on her face. "What are you thinking about?" She put her head to the side, studying him as she spoke.

He held back a chuckle. Nothing was going to get past his new wife. "I was wondering about you. Just my curiosity getting the better of me, I guess."

"There should be some mystery between us, no?" She continued to study him, then grinned. "I am teasing you. It will come with time. Now I should like some coffee before we go home."

She winked at him, and it conjured up all sorts of scenarios in McKenzie's mind. One thing he knew for certain – he would never tire of looking at his wife. She was beautiful in more ways than one, proving that in Verity's case, beauty was not only skin deep.

After they left the diner, McKenzie took her arm and escorted his new wife around the town of Carson's Hollow. He was proud to be seen with such a beauty on his arm and pointed out the various stores she would likely visit. "It's not a large town by any means," he said as they continued to wander. "But it's enough for the locals. Besides, it's too far to travel to the next largest town, which is hours away." McKenzie felt her stiffen. "Anything you need can be ordered via the mercantile."

"That makes me harder to find, yes?"

Her question had him curious. She wasn't in hiding. Or was she? "Are you worried about your uncle? Because if you are…."

"I don't think he would come after me, but he won't be happy about the jewelry he says is his."

That put McKenzie on alert. He should have already realized it was a possibility from what Verity had said earlier. The man was selfish and greedy and wouldn't care if it was his property or not. Without even knowing him personally, McKenzie decided he was the sort of individual who would take what he wanted, no matter what. "Tomorrow, we will visit the solicitor and sort out ownership of the jewelry and everything else. That way, we'll know once and for all."

Verity nodded and her features softened. It was apparent she was worried about her uncle turning up unannounced, so McKenzie would keep an eye out. The man sounded like someone he needed to worry about.

"Shall we head for home?"

"If you wish," Verity said softly. "I want to be a good wife to you, McKenzie, but I'm not sure how."

Her words made him pause. Perhaps she did have a sheltered life after all. She shivered as they rounded the corner toward the sheriff's house. "You're cold." He stopped and removed his jacket, placing it over her shoulders.

"Now you will be cold," she said softly.

He glanced down into her moonlit face. "I'm a big boy; I can take it." He chuckled, and rubbed a hand across his bristly face, then placed his arm across her shoulders. "I think once you get used to it, you'll love Carson's Hollow. There is little drama, and the people are friendly. Of course, we have our town drunk and fights at the saloon, but that's about it."

"No uncles coming to claim jewelry that doesn't belong to them?" She smiled tentatively, and McKenzie knew she was trying to make light of the situation. Unfortunately, it could turn out to be a serious situation, but he had no intention of saying so.

"Hopefully, we'll clear that up tomorrow." He squeezed her hand, When they arrived home, he unlocked the door and pondered the days ahead. Two strangers thrown together in a difficult situation. At least for Verity, it was difficult. For McKenzie, nothing much had changed, except maybe, if he was lucky, his bed might be a little warmer tonight.

~*~

Verity stared at her reflection in the bathroom mirror. Was she really married to this gentle, caring man? Being a sheriff, she expected him to be more rough and tumble, and perhaps even a bit gruff. But he was none of that.

He seemed genuinely worried about her uncle turning up and was keen to have the legalities of her jewelry and other possessions checked. At least as much as Verity was. She'd changed into her linen nightgown and couldn't put off the inevitable any longer. She was McKenzie's wife and needed to go to his bed.

Oh, he was every bit the gentleman and had offered to let her sleep in the spare room if that was what she wanted, but right now it was full of her as yet unpacked belongings. Besides, she might as well get it over with instead of worrying about becoming his wife in every way. She put down her brush, glancing for the last time at herself as an innocent bride, then quickly left the bathroom. She took a deep breath and let it out slowly as she made her way to the bedroom. It was now or never.

She quickly went into the small room. Well, small compared to what she had back home. McKenzie's entire house could fit in her Ontario bedroom. She closed her eyes momentarily. All thought of home needed to go. This was home now – Carson's Hollow. McKenzie was her husband, and where he went, she would follow.

On opening her eyes again, she saw the room was empty and let out the breath Verity didn't realize she was holding. She gasped as a large hand slipped around her waist. "You startled me," she said quietly.

McKenzie pulled her against him. "I'm sorry, I didn't mean to scare you." Suddenly he began to nibble her neck. "Are you sure about this? I mean…the offer of the spare room is still there."

She shook her head, and he lifted her gently off her feet and carried his new wife to their marital bed. She couldn't help but stare as McKenzie removed first his shirt, then his belt and pants. She stared at the beauty of this man, her husband. She gulped at the muscles in his arms, the muscles that were undetectable under his jacket. Last of all, he removed his drawers, and she averted her eyes. She heard him chuckle, then moments later, the bed dipped as he climbed in next to her. He pulled her close and wrapped his big arms around her. His warmth seeped into her, and despite her reservations, she wasn't scared. McKenzie's touch reassured her.

It wasn't long before his body covered hers, and she was Mrs. McKenzie Dunn in every way.

"Tell me about each individual piece of jewelry." Town solicitor Henry Siringo studied Verity as he spoke.

McKenzie could see she was nervous; her hands shook, even as they sat in her lap. "Most of it belonged to my mother. I inherited it when she died – it was in her Will it should come to me. The rest were gifts from my father."

He smiled. "I will request a copy of your mother's will to verify. The rest will be difficult to prove."

Verity dipped her head. McKenzie could see she was upset, but there was little he could do about it. "Oh," she suddenly brought her head up again. "Father always used the same jeweler in Ontario and had the items delivered as gifts. Would that help?"

Henry grinned. "Most definitely." He scribbled some notes as she spoke, including details of the jewelry shop. "Might I suggest you place all your jewelry here for safe-keeping? At least until I am able to verify ownership? That way, if your uncle does turn up, he cannot get his hands on your treasured possessions."

McKenzie clapped his hands together. "That's an excellent idea, Henry," he said, delighted at the prospect. He reached across to Verity and took her hand in his. She was still shaking, and he wasn't sure how he could console her. "Thank you for your advice. I was certain you would know what to do about this situation."

"As for the crockery," Henry continued, "Why would he even want that?" He seemed as perplexed as McKenzie was.

"Out of spite. He is a vindictive man, my Uncle Louis." She pursed her lips, and her anger was palpable. "Oh, that is in my mother's will too. Everything except my clothing is in the will or should be noted at the jewelry shop."

Henry rubbed his hands together. "Excellent," he said, then stood. "I'll be in touch as soon as I hear anything. In the meantime, bring your jewelry here for safe-keeping."

Verity glanced at McKenzie. Was she feeling uncertain? The last person she needed to worry about was Henry Siringo; he was as trustworthy as they came.

"I will, of course, provide a receipt for each item stored."

Her relief was evident at his words. "Thank you," she said in that sweet voice of hers. He guided her to the door, and they went straight back home, where they packed up every piece of jewelry, then McKenzie took it straight back to Henry. He had no doubt Louis LeFebvre would turn up in Carson's Hollow sooner rather than later to claim what he believed to be rightfully his. At least what he pretended to believe was rightfully his.

McKenzie waited while Henry itemized each piece, then handed him a receipt. Verity was at the mercantile shopping. "Can I ask you to do one more thing, now that my wife isn't here?"

Henry stared at him curiously. "Go on."

"I'd like the father's will verified. I find it difficult to believe Pierre LeFebvre completely cut his only child out of his will."

"Done."

"Let me pay your fee upfront, Henry. I don't want you out of pocket. I'm sure there will be fees to retrieve all this information."

Henry brushed McKenzie's words aside. "I know you're good for it. This uncle, he seems rather an er, fraudster, don't you think?"

"I do think. It appears Verity has never laid eyes on her father's will, so I'd like confirmation it's all above board. I don't think the money is important to her, but she has lost everything she ever had. Clothes, friends, stability. According to Louis, he was willed everything."

Henry's eyebrows crinkled. "Everything?"

"Absolutely everything – the house and the property it stands on, all his possessions, as well as his booming railway business. According to Louis, Verity was left homeless and penniless."

Henry stared at him for long moments. "We'll see about that," he said between clenched teeth.

As he left the solicitor's office, McKenzie heard him curse under his breath.

Chapter Three

Verity lay in bed as though she were a lady of leisure. Only that wasn't what she was anymore. She was the sheriff's wife, and surely there must be something she should be doing?

She listened carefully as she heard shuffling feet moving about in the house and prayed it was McKenzie, and not her uncle come to accost her. She quietly got out of bed and slinked through the house, trying not to be heard. At the end of the passageway, she gingerly put her head around the corner toward the sound and was relieved to see her husband standing there.

He glanced up when he saw her and smiled. "Good morning, Mrs. Dunn." He shook the onions in the frypan but made no attempt to come to her. "Can't leave these, or they might burn," he said, a touch of sadness on his face.

She stepped toward him, and his free arm snaked around her shoulders. McKenzie leaned in and kissed her tenderly. Removing his arm, he threw the bacon and eggs into the pan. As though he hadn't noticed her before, he stared long and hard at her. It was then Verity realized she stood in the middle of the kitchen, almost naked.

Well, not really naked, but she did only wear her nightgown and nothing else. She felt the heat crawl up her neck and onto her face, where it continued to climb. McKenzie laughed, which annoyed her to no end.

"I, I'll just go and get my robe," she said, but he was having none of it.

"Have a seat. I'm about to dish up."

He pulled down two plates from the overhead cupboard and retrieved the toast from the oven where it was keeping hot. He plated everything up, then placed her breakfast in front of Verity. She leaned in and breathed in the intoxicating aroma of breakfast. Her husband was spoiling her, but from now on, it was she who needed to spoil him. "It smells wonderful," she said as he placed a mug of coffee in front of her.

He took his place at the table, then reached for her hand. "Holy Father, bless this food, this house, and the people in it. Amen."

Verity smiled. It had been a long time since she'd been at a table where a blessing was said. Uncle Louis wouldn't allow it in *his* house, which was confusing as his mission was said to be spreading the word of God. Her father was a devout Christian, and so was Verity. It cut through her sensibilities to have that part of her life banished. Instead of arguing, which she'd done in the beginning without result, she silently said the blessing in her head.

"Tomorrow, I'll get up before you and cook the breakfast." Verity tucked into her food. "This is really good. Where did you learn to cook?"

McKenzie chuckled. "This is pretty much my entire repertoire. It was cook or starve. Sometimes I have to go away for days. Then I have to cook on an open fire."

Her heart sank. Did that mean her husband would leave her for days at a time? She hoped not, but if it was part of his job, there was nothing she could do about it. She glanced up to see him staring at her.

"What are you thinking?"

Should she tell him or keep her concerns to herself? McKenzie's hand reached across and covered hers. He gave it a gentle squeeze, and a shiver ran down her spine. "How often do you have to go away?" Her voice was quiet, only slightly above a whisper.

He pulled his hand back and took a gulp of coffee. "Not often, but it does happen from time to time. Are you worried you'll miss me?" His last words sounded flirty, which she hadn't expected. Nonetheless, it made her smile.

"Miss you? Why would I do that?" Strange as it seemed, Verity knew she would miss her husband if he wasn't there. He was her gentle giant, and she imagined he'd be a force to be reckoned with when the occasion called for it.

He grinned, then went back to his food, which he finished in silence. He went to pick up his soiled dishes, but Verity stopped him. "That's my job now." He nodded, then leaned in and kissed her forehead.

"I have to go now, but if circumstances permit, I will be home for lunch. Any supplies you need, put on my account at the mercantile."

"I doubt I'll need anything else yet since I went there yesterday. I'll probably spend most of the day unpacking, if that's all right with you."

McKenzie nodded his agreement. "If you need me, you'll likely find me at the Sheriff's Office." He began to walk away but turned back, pulling Verity to her feet. He enveloped her with his strong arms and kissed her tenderly. He finally dropped his arms and slowly walked away.

Verity stared after him; it seemed crazy since they barely knew each other, but she missed him already.

McKenzie leaned back in his well-worn chair in the Sheriff's Office. He had been thinking about Verity all morning when he should be working and had to get her off his mind. He had work to do; this couldn't continue.

The door suddenly opened, and his wife strode through. It was as though he'd conjured her up through his thoughts. He couldn't help but smile. "I didn't expect to see you here today. How is the unpacking going?" Surely he could think of something more creative to say?

Verity smiled back. "It's going well. I got a bit tired, is all, and decided it was time for a break." She twisted her hands in front of her as though there was something she wanted to say but just couldn't come out with it.

"Is something wrong, Verity?"

She stared at him but didn't say a word. Was her uncle in town? McKenzie certainly hoped not. He came around to the other side of the desk and pulled her close. "Tell me what's bothering you. I'm your husband, and if you hadn't noticed, I'm also the sheriff." He grinned at her, trying to make light of the situation. Verity stared up at him, then shook her head.

"It's nothing like that," she said. "It's just... I don't know what you like to eat." She glanced up at him. "I told you I'm not the best of cooks. I made thick vegetable soup for lunch and some freshly baked bread. I've only made bread once before, so I hope it turns out all right."

He stared at her for a moment, then chuckled. "I was beginning to think it was something serious. Honestly, I'll eat anything you put in front of me." He leaned in and kissed her forehead. McKenzie knew he shouldn't feel this way, but he didn't want her to leave. He'd been fiddling about with paperwork all morning when what he should have been doing was his rounds. Checking on the store owners and making sure everything was all right with them.

Much of his job consisted of walking around town, keeping the peace, and locking up drunks and thieves. Of course, he would prefer to be with Verity, but that's not what he was being paid to do. "I will walk you back home." He glanced down at her, but her face gave nothing away. "If that's where you want to go. I need to stretch my legs anyway."

She nodded but said not a word. It would be a good hour before he could go home for lunch. Most days, he skipped eating, but that wasn't an option now.

Verity would expect him to have lunch, except when he wasn't in a position to do so.

He waited while she unlocked the door and went inside. He tucked his head around the door, and the aroma was enticing. "Smells good." Too bad he had to go back to work now.

She went straight to the stove and stirred the pot. "I hope it tastes as good as it smells."

McKenzie was sure it would. "I really have to go now," he said but checked the other rooms before he left. He was convinced her uncle wouldn't get here this soon if he intended to confront Verity, but you just never knew. Did he even know where she was? It was another question for McKenzie to verify. If Louis had fiddled with the will, or covered up the contents, which was far more likely, then he was capable of anything.

He wrapped his arms around Verity and kissed her cheek. If he kissed her lips, he knew he would have far too much trouble leaving her. It might only be an hour or so before he returned, but he already knew it would feel more like a lifetime.

He reluctantly left his wife alone and returned to his work.

The saloon was the bane of McKenzie's life. He spent more time keeping the peace there than anywhere else in town. He'd practically begged the Mayor to bring in a law, keeping the saloon closed until at least three in the afternoon, but he blankly refused. He cited profits as well as workers losing money. Of course, the lost taxes to the town would be high on his agenda.

McKenzie sighed and headed to the saloon. He pushed the doors open and stood in the doorway, staring across the room. Marty Jones stood behind the bar as he always did, pouring beer and whiskey, oblivious to what was going on around him. Charlie Hanson sat at the bar, if you could call it sitting. The man was stooped over as he slurped down the last of his whiskey. McKenzie had locked him up far more times than he cared to remember.

He wasn't violent, and he never got nasty, but he was jailed for his own protection. When he got like this, some of the other drinkers took advantage, stealing money from his wallet while Charlie slept it off where he sat.

"Come on, Charlie," he said as he grabbed the other man's arm. "There's a comfortable bed waiting for you at the jailhouse."

The old man glanced up momentarily and nodded his thanks. It was a scenario McKenzie had seen far too many times now. Oh, he always charged those miserable thieves if he caught them, but he was sure they got away with it far more times than they'd been arrested, so the stealing continued. Much to his disgust.

He supported Charlie as he walked him back to the Sheriff's Office. Thank goodness it wasn't far away. Charlie needed a long, hot bath and some clean clothes. His house, if you could call it that, was falling down around the old man, but there was nothing he could do about it. The cottage had been there since Carson's Hollow had been established, close to a century ago. If the place had been maintained, it might have been a different story, but with the old man's drinking habits, that was never going to happen. He only survived because of his long-time workers, who refused to give up. They kept the farm going, took out their wages, and handed the rest over to Charlie. More's the pity. If he had no money to spend, he might dry out.

Charlie Hanson had been a decent citizen until the love of his life had died some years back. They had no children, none that survived anyway, and now he was alone with no one to help him out of his dreadful situation.

McKenzie shook his head. It wasn't his problem. At least that's what everyone told him. He'd known old Charlie all his life and had a soft spot for the man.

"Here we go, Charlie," he said, helping his 'prisoner' into the cell. "My new missus has made soup for lunch. I'll see if I can rustle up some food for you a bit later." Otherwise, he'd get a meal from the diner.

Charlie raised his hand for about ten seconds, then laid back on the pillow. He was sound asleep before McKenzie had closed the door to the cell.

He'd no sooner returned to his office than the door flew open. "Mail's in." The postmaster handed him a large envelope and left as quickly as he'd arrived.

More Wanted posters. Just what he needed. McKenzie sighed. There was a constant flow of criminals and a never ending supply of new *Wanted* posters. He could barely keep up. He added this latest batch to those already pinned to the wall and looked them over. A few stagecoach robbers, a couple of thieves and bank robbers, and the rest were wanted for murder or assault.

It must surely be time to eat? His stomach was telling him it was, so McKenzie locked up the Sheriff's Office and strolled home to his new wife and her delicious smelling food.

Verity stood at the stove, stirring the soup. She slowly turned as he entered but looked far from happy.

"What's wrong?" She looked on the verge of tears, and it broke his heart.

"I ruined it. And the bread – I think it's going to be horrid."

She did say she wasn't the best cook, but surely the food was salvageable? He stepped toward her and put an arm around her shoulder, hoping to comfort his wife. She glanced up at him, tears shimmering in her eyes. He needed to reassure her. "I'm sure it will be fine."

Verity pushed the bread toward him. "Would you mind cutting this?"

McKenzie picked up the knife already sitting on the board and cut into the bread. At least he tried to cut into it. Firm was an understatement; rock hard was a far better description. "This knife obviously needs sharpening," he said gently, not wanting to upset her further. "I can do without bread today."

She nodded and pulled in her bottom lip, turning away from him again. McKenzie hoped, for Verity's sake, the soup was edible. She no doubt spent a considerable amount of time on it already. She reached for two bowls and dished out a more than generous amount for him and placed it on the table in front of him. McKenzie stared at it. *What if it was inedible?* She sat down opposite him, and he said the blessing before they began to eat.

He gingerly dipped his spoon into the food in front of him and took a mouthful. "It needs salt," he said as she stared at him, waiting for his assessment of her cooking. McKenzie wasn't certain they had enough salt to fix it, but he had no intention of upsetting his bride further. "Did you put any pepper in it? I think it needs some of that too."

"I added a few herbs but didn't think to add salt and pepper."

"Ah, that will be it then." He ground pepper into his meal and tried not to grimace. It was the worst soup he'd ever had the misfortune to taste but would never say it out loud.

"It's terrible, isn't it?" A tear slid down her face, and she swiped at it. What was he supposed to do now? He couldn't bear to see his wife upset and didn't want to admit the truth to her, but it was truly inedible. Verity lifted her spoon and took a mouthful. "Oh my gosh," she sputtered. "This is truly awful. Why didn't you say something?" Without waiting for another word, she removed the offending food from in front of him and threw it outside on the vegetable patch.

Verity turned her back on him, and he was sure she was crying, although she didn't let on to him if she was. He went to her side and pulled her into his arms. "It doesn't matter. Let's go to the diner for lunch. We'll work something out for supper."

She leaned against his chest, and he could see she was truly devastated. Served himself right for sending for a bride to have home-cooked food. Only

McKenzie knew that wasn't really true. Sure he wanted home cooked meals, and he could get those at the diner. What he really wanted was someone special to share his life with. To eradicate the loneliness he often felt coming home to an empty house. He wanted what his friends, Sarah and Luke Carson had – a deep and meaningful relationship. Love. Family. And everything that went with it.

He wanted someone to truly love and cherish. He hoped that person was Verity.

She glanced up at him, tears still shimmering in her eyes. "Really? You're not mad at me?"

It made him pause. Is that what happened with her uncle when she couldn't cook decent food? He got mad? He hated to think of him physically abusing her. "I'm not mad, far from it. I know of plenty of brides who have buried their cooking failures."

She raised her eyebrows. "Surely not."

"It's true, I swear." He pulled her a little tighter and wrapped her in his warmth. His wife had been through far more grief and stress than anyone deserved. He vowed not to be yet another source of despair for her and led her out the door and toward the diner. She didn't complain.

Chapter Four

Lunch was good, and McKenzie wasn't even mad at her. By now, Uncle Louis would be throwing a major tantrum because she'd taken everything that legally belonged to Verity. At least she believed they did. McKenzie's solicitor would sort it out, which made her feel far better.

After Marguerite, their cook, had died, it had fallen on Verity to prepare all the meals. Only she wasn't good at it.

As a result, they ate basic food, which didn't go down well with her uncle. He was, of course, too stingy to employ another cook. After all, Marguerite worked for board and lodgings and a small stipend. They both knew that wouldn't happen again.

Verity cooked only what she had learned from Marguerite, which wasn't a lot – scrambled eggs, bacon and eggs, and a few other simple dishes.

What she really needed was cooking lessons, but where could she do that here in Carson's Hollow? She could ask Jeannie here at the diner, but she made money from people buying her meals. Why would she encourage someone to cook for themselves?

It was a ridiculous idea, and she needed to push it to the back of her mind.

They were about to leave when McKenzie remembered something. "I almost forgot – I need a meal for Charlie."

Jeannie rolled her eyes. "I sincerely wish Charlie would stop drinking. Wait here."

"Charlie?" Verity had no idea who they were talking about.

"Unfortunately, he's the town drunk," her husband explained. "He's sitting in a cell right now. I have to feed him."

She grimaced. "And I ruined the soup."

He reached out and squeezed her hand. "It's not a big deal. Jeannie has been supplying the jailhouse meals for years." He glanced down at her. "Besides, if you start supplying meals, she'll lose that income."

His words made her feel a little better, even if it didn't negate the fact that she was an awful cook.

Jeannie returned with a tray that was covered with a kitchen towel. "Here you are – thick vegetable soup and freshly baked biscuits. There's also some rice pudding, and I've added a mug of strong black coffee. No doubt, dear old Charlie needs to sober up."

"Thanks Jeannie, you're a sweetheart." Verity watched as heat crept up the other woman's face.

McKenzie took the tray, and they headed to the jail. "This won't take long, and then I can walk you home."

She unlocked the door to the Sheriff's Office at McKenzie's request, and the food was delivered. "I can walk home alone, you know," she said quietly as they were about to leave. "Do you think Jeannie would teach me to cook?" His eyes never left her face, and it made her squirm. "It's a silly idea, I guess."

"No, it's a brilliant idea. Tell her I am offering to pay for the lessons." His eyes suddenly sparkled as though the thought of decent food filled him with delight. Truth be known, it probably did; wasn't the way to a man's heart through his belly? At least that's what she'd heard. It was a pity they didn't teach cooking at that over-priced finishing school she'd attended. It had cost her father a fortune yet was useless in the real world.

Sure, Verity could hold her head high, could fashion her hair, could pick fashionable clothes. But it didn't fill her husband's belly with good food.

He leaned in and kissed her tenderly. Was that McKenzie's way of telling her it was time to go? She figured it was. "I, um…what should I do about supper?" She was embarrassed to ask, but she needed to plan ahead.

He chucked her under the chin. "Tell Jeannie we'll be there for supper." He leaned in and kissed her again. "Now go. You are far too much of a distraction, and I have work to do." He grinned as he straightened, and she turned away.

Too much of a distraction, eh? At least she had one thing going for her.

She hurried up the road toward the diner and slipped inside. Jeannie was nowhere in sight, and thankfully there were no customers. It was almost empty when she and McKenzie had eaten there, and more so now. She glanced about. There were around twenty tables, and Verity wondered if they were ever all full. How busy did the diner get?

"Verity! You're back." Jeannie stared at her for long moments. "Is there something I can help you with?"

"Yes, there is. At least I hope you can help." She twisted her hands in front of her, a bad habit she picked up some years ago. Father tried to get her out of it, but it didn't happen.

Jeannie watched her but didn't say a word.

"I need cooking lessons. Can you teach me?"

Jeannie chuckled. "You can't be that bad of a cook." Despite her words, she continued to stare.

"Our lunch ended up on the vegetable patch. The soup was spoiled, and McKenzie couldn't even cut the bread with the sharpest knife in the house." She glanced down at the floor in shame.

"Oh." *Oh indeed.* It was probably the best way to describe her attempts. "Well then, I'm sure I can help. Why did you attempt bread? It is one of the hardest things to master."

She glanced up to watch the other woman. "I wanted to make my husband glad he married me."

Verity thought she heard Jeannie sigh. "McKenzie is easy to please, so he won't hold it against you, I'm certain. The kitchen is this way," she said, hurrying off. Verity had no choice but to follow.

She'd never made muffins before, but Verity had mastered them. At least that's what Jeannie told her. They began with basics, with Jeannie teaching her how to separate eggs, mix milk into flour without making it lumpy, and a few other things. She promised to teach Verity something new every day.

Jeannie and Verity ate one of her still warm blueberry muffins, and if she did say so herself, it was very nice. So nice, in fact, Jeannie gave her one to take to her husband. She also sent one for dear old Charlie.

McKenzie couldn't believe she'd made it herself. "You made this?" His voice was incredulous, and his expression matched.

Well, she sort of did. Jeannie gave her step by step instructions and totally supervised, but Verity had done all the work. Oh, she knew very well she couldn't replicate it at home. Not yet, and probably not for a very long time, but the fact she'd managed to make something edible and make her husband proud was all she needed right now. "I surprised myself. Jeannie is a terrific teacher."

"Well, it's delicious. Tell Jeannie I said thanks." He reached out and grabbed her hand as Verity turned to leave. "You know I don't care if you can't cook?"

He sounded genuine, but Verity thought otherwise. All men wanted their wives to be able to cook a decent meal. Jeannie promised to teach her everything she knew, which would probably take quite some time. It didn't bother Verity – after all, what else was she to do with her time?

She quickly returned to the diner where she'd promised to help Jeannie with the evening preparation. Apart from McKenzie and herself, there were six other tables booked, plus those who might arrive without bookings.

Her next job today was to cut the meat and cover it with flour, ready for the stew. Her mentor showed Verity how to cut the meat – all in cubes of around the same size, so it cooked evenly. Once that was done, she added it to the griddle to seal the meat and give it a lovely appearance. Then it went into a large pot on the huge wood stove Jeannie had in her kitchen. She added sliced onions to brown, then added water.

Once that was done, they began to prepare the vegetables. It was tedious work, but she was learning by doing. Verity pushed a stray bit of hair back off her face. She hadn't worked this hard for a very long time and wondered how Jeannie did this day in and day out alone. No wonder she was quick to take up Verity's request to work with her, despite her lack of experience.

The two chatted as they worked. When asked, Verity told the older woman how she came to be in Carson's Hollow. Jeannie was, of course, sorry she'd been through that but said she was glad Verity had married McKenzie. She stopped what she was doing and studied Verity. "He's been lonely for a very long time. But he's a stubborn man and refused to give in and find a wife." She brushed back a stray piece of hair before speaking again. "I'm glad he waited. Otherwise, he wouldn't have married you."

The sincere words made her feel warm and fuzzy all over. Verity was glad she'd married him too. He was a good man, caring and kind. She could have ended up with anyone, but she'd been matched with a decent, law-abiding man. One who, despite only knowing him for a matter of days, looked out for her and ensured the only things she truly treasured were kept safe from harm. And from her uncle.

Verity glanced up at Jeannie. The other woman was studying her. "Are you all right, my dear? You have gone white."

"Have I?" The fact surprised her. "I was thinking about my horrid uncle."

Jeannie pulled out a chair. "Sit down for a moment. I'll make you a nice cup of tea. Perhaps we should have a break, anyway; we've been working non-stop for quite some time."

Verity brushed her mentor's words aside. "I'm fine, I promise. Just thinking about him sends shivers down my spine. And not in a nice way." She glanced up momentarily. Would Jeannie think badly of her? "Ordinarily, I wouldn't fight over possessions. But my mother's jewelry is all I have left of her." She swallowed down the emotion that threatened to overtake her.

A hand reached out and covered hers. "Of course. I'm very pleased McKenzie had the foresight to consult with Henry. He'll keep your possessions safe."

Verity nodded, then the two women went back to what they were previously doing – preparing vegetables for the evening's meals.

Verity had not long finished cleaning herself up after a hard day working at the diner when her husband arrived home. He looked tired, and it made her feel guilty. If not for her, he would be able to have a restful night at home. Instead, she had him gallivanting off to the diner to eat. *What sort of wife was she?*

Instead of castigating her, McKenzie wrapped her in his arms. "How was your day?" he asked, seeming genuinely interested.

She stared up into his tired face. "It was good. Hard work and I'm sure I'll forget most of what I learned today, but Jeannie really needs help. I'm glad I was able to do that."

A hand reached up and caressed her cheek. "You're a good person, Verity." He leaned in and gently brushed her lips with his own. He pulled back quickly, and she knew he was trying to keep himself in check. She felt the same way – McKenzie made her feel things she had no right to feel. It made her wonder if he felt the same or whether it was just the way men were. Wanting their manly rights, but knowing there were other priorities right at that moment.

She leaned against him. Verity felt protected and cared for whenever McKenzie was around. He was a big man, but that wasn't the reason. He looked out for her. There was no doubt about it, but he seemed quite genuine in his actions. They were virtual strangers, and she could barely believe only two days ago, they hadn't even met. Now it felt as though they'd known each other forever. Had her presence affected him the way he affected her?

She felt his arms tighten around her. Warmth flooded her. "Are you all right?" His words brought her out of her thoughts, and heat flooded her face. He gently lifted her chin with his fingers.

Verity nodded. "Just thinking silly things." She glanced up at him and stared into his chocolate colored eyes.

He leaned in and kissed her again, and instead of going to the diner to eat, Verity wanted to stay right where she was.

Chapter Five

McKenzie wiped his lips with the napkin. "That was delicious. I can safely say you *are* a great cook."

Verity frowned. "Jeannie must take all the credit. I only followed her instructions and didn't do a lot."

"I heard otherwise. You're a fast learner, according to Jeannie." He lifted his mug and gulped down his coffee. "That tastes wonderful."

She stared down into her lap. "I'll learn how to make decent coffee too, I suspect."

He glanced at her. Did his wife think that was a criticism because it wasn't? "Your coffee is fine. These things all take time. Don't be so tough on yourself." He reached across the table and covered her hand with his own. "With your background, no one blames you for not knowing these things." She scowled at him, but McKenzie wasn't sure why. After all, what he said was the truth. Then again, sometimes the truth hurt, and the last thing he wanted to do was hurt Verity.

"How was your meal?" Jeannie interrupted them just in time.

"It was delicious as always."

His coffee mug was refilled without asking. "What's for dessert tonight?"

"Apple pie, blueberry muffins," She winked at him, presumably because he'd already sampled the muffins. "And rice pudding."

"I'll have the apple pie, thank you. What about you, Verity?"

She glanced up at Jeannie. "I'll have the pie too, thank you." She took a sip of her coffee as their hostess walked away. "I feel like I should be helping her. It's such a busy place, and she does it all alone."

His grip tightened on her hand. "I'm certain Jeannie appreciates the help you're giving her during the day." McKenzie was positive it would be the case. He couldn't recall her ever having assistance in the diner. Verity's help would be a godsend to her.

"You're right, of course. I'm pleased to be able to help. At first, I thought I might be a hindrance, but Jeannie said it was a massive help."

"Of course, it was. She would be very grateful to you."

"Here you are. Two apple pies." Jeannie put the bowls down, one in front of each of them.

"Verity thinks she was a hindrance in the kitchen today." His wife glared at him as heat rose in her cheeks.

Jeannie's head shot up. "My dear girl, you were far from that. Today was the first time in ages I haven't been stressing the entire day, trying to get everything done."

"I'm pleased to hear it," Verity said quietly. He'd embarrassed her, but it was better than having her feel guilty for no reason.

"Tuck in," Jeannie said, then left them alone. McKenzie waited for his wife to admonish him, but her words never came. He didn't take her for a wallflower, so he was pleased to have appeased her guilty thoughts.

After supper, they went for a stroll around town. Despite his deputy, Matt Collier, doing the night duty, he went to the jailhouse to check on Charlie, who was still sleeping it off. The old man was fine – he'd had an early supper before McKenzie collected Verity. He ate better in jail than he did at home and was never in a hurry to leave.

It was always at the back of his mind to find a way to help Charlie, but what do you do when that help is not wanted? It was a problem for another day.

"Everything all right, Matt?" he asked as they were leaving. "No problems to report?"

"No problems, Sheriff."

It was as he expected. Carson's Hollow was a quiet town with mostly law-abiding citizens. Newcomers stood out like a sore thumb, and McKenzie always kept an eye on them until he could be certain they weren't there to cause trouble. Troublemakers like Louis LeFebvre. He dreaded the day that man arrived. Oh, McKenzie knew the day would come – he just hoped by then Henry had all the legalities sorted out. How long that would take, he wasn't sure, but he wanted it over with quickly, for Verity's sake.

At least he knew her treasured possessions were safe from harm and from Louis' greedy hands.

They walked along the boardwalk, and he pointed out some of the more exclusive stores to his wife. "This is the boutique where the rich ladies buy their gowns." Verity stared at him and swallowed. "I didn't mean…."

"It's all right. I know you didn't."

He quickly moved to the next store. "This is our boot maker. Without this store, we would have to travel to get our boots." He lifted one leg to show her his boot. "These came from there. Tom is the best for miles around. His boots last for years."

They moved on and headed home, the moon shining brightly above them. "I love it here." Verity's words were muted. "It is so peaceful. Back home, it was always busy. Father was always rushing here and there, meetings to attend, places to be. I hated it." She twisted her hands in front of her. "I barely got to see him after we lost Mother. And then he died." Her last words were barely audible, and McKenzie put his arm to her shoulders and pulled her close.

"I'm really sorry," he said gently, and he truly was. That his wife was unhappy made him feel that way too. McKenzie hoped her sadness would leave her when she had been here for a while and settled in. If he could eliminate her worries about her uncle, he would be ecstatic.

They finally arrived home, where he unlocked the door and led her inside. In the privacy of their home, he took her in his arms to comfort her. Verity leaned against his chest and sighed. They stood that way for what seemed like a lifetime.

Verity finished fashioning her hair atop her head, then added a bonnet. Apart from the day they married, this would be her first foray to the Carson's Hollow church. Despite being excited to meet some of the townsfolk, she was nervous. What would they think of her? She worried they would see her as the failed daughter of a wealthy railway owner.

It wasn't her fault her parents were now both gone, that her uncle had inherited everything, and she had lost far more than she ever thought possible. Even her prized possessions, her mother's jewelry, were locked up where she couldn't touch it. Oh, she knew she couldn't wear it – the jewelry was totally unsuitable for her new environment, but simply touching it made her feel closer to her mother. It brought back many happy memories, and she didn't want those memories to fade.

Now she couldn't even do that, and all because her uncle was greedy and uncaring. According to her father, he was never like that, and she wondered what had caused the change in him. Father would be appalled.

"Are you almost ready? We need to go or risk being late." McKenzie's voice brought her out of her wayward thoughts. Verity knew it was no good focusing on things she couldn't change and needed to move forward. Despite that, it was difficult letting go of the past, especially when there was so much bitterness involved.

"I think so." She snatched up her reticle and brushed her hands down her skirt one last time. Not that it was wrinkled – it was perfect. Her apprehension was rattling her nerves.

McKenzie came up behind her and put an arm around her shoulder. "Relax. We're going to church, not the ball of the century." He smiled, trying to put her at ease.

Thinking about it, Verity realized she'd been equally nervous preparing for those balls. To be truthful, she'd hated them. She was paraded about like a piece of meat. Her father was keen to see her married and happy and with a brood of children. Heirs to his vast empire.

All of the men who took any interest in her were only after her father's money, and that was the last thing Verity wanted. Gold diggers – she hated the thought. In the end, she refused to attend anything that portrayed her as looking for a groom, suitable or not.

She had purposely not divulged details of her father or his fortune when applying to be a mail order bride. She didn't want a prospective groom to accept her, thinking he would have an easy life or get his hands on riches. Not that it was ever going to happen. Her greedy uncle had seen to that.

They stepped outside the front door, and Verity breathed in the fresh air. She truly loved Carson's Hollow. The people were lovely, and it was peaceful. So far, everyone had been nice to her, but she had yet to meet the bulk of the townsfolk.

She hooked her arm through McKenzie's, and they headed toward the church. The closer they got, the clearer she could hear the organ playing. Her heart fluttered at the thought of sitting in the House of God, where she always felt totally at home. If there was one place she knew she fit in, despite her upbringing, it was there.

As they stepped inside, all her worries seemed to disappear.

Sipping on a mug of tea, Verity looked about. She recognized the handful of people she'd already met, mostly store owners. Jeannie was there, along with Arthur and Flo from the mercantile. McKenzie introduced her to his friends, Luke and Sarah Carson. They had two young children with them. She met Luke's workers too, but she couldn't remember their names. Names were never her strong point, and today had proven that point. Surely no one would expect her to remember names for everyone she'd met?

As people went home and the room thinned, she felt far more comfortable in her surroundings. Her expensive clothes didn't help. It was then she decided to ask McKenzie if she could get some gowns from the mercantile. At least that way, she would fit in more and not stand out. She was about to stand up when someone sat down beside her. It was Sarah Carson. She balanced a small child on her lap.

"I hope you're settling in. It's not easy being a mail order bride." Verity glanced up at her questionably. "I was a mail order bride too. It was the best thing I ever did."

Verity nodded slightly. "It's been difficult." She glanced down at her hands that were twisting in her lap. "McKenzie is lovely, don't get me wrong. It's just so different here to what I'm used to."

Sarah reached over and covered her hands. "I know. It was hard for me too, but probably not in the same way it is for you." She stared across the room at McKenzie. "Your husband is a wonderful man. I haven't known him long, but from what I've seen, he has been lonely for far too long. He needed a wife."

Verity knew what Sarah said was true. McKenzie had admitted as much himself. "I know, but I'm not a good wife. I can't even cook, but Jeannie is teaching me." She stared down at her hands again. "I feel that I've failed him. He wanted someone who could cook, and I can't."

Sarah's arm went up around her shoulders, and Verity felt somewhat comforted. "He doesn't care about that," she said quietly. "He is already very fond of you. He told me so himself."

Verity's heart fluttered. She hoped it was true; she was very fond of McKenzie too.

"It's nice to see you two getting along." Her husband's voice brought her back to reality. "Are you ready to leave?" He helped Verity to her feet, and they made their way home.

After a nice roast lunch at the diner, McKenzie suggested an afternoon exploring the area. Verity hadn't seen much of Carson's Hollow and agreed. They would go up into the hills and let her see the town from above and drive around for a relaxing afternoon. It sounded wonderful.

If she'd known ahead, she could have prepared a picnic lunch. She knew how to make sandwiches, even if it did mean buying a loaf of bread. She could have bought some muffins from the diner, and that would have got them through. She sighed. Perhaps another time.

They strolled down to the livery, where McKenzie hired a buggy. It was a pleasant day, but despite that, he'd taken a blanket to place across their legs. It could get quite cool up in the hills, he'd told her. He helped her up into the buggy, and they were soon on their way. It was a pleasant drive out of town and seemed like forever before they began to work their way through the nearby hills. Hollow Mountains seemed a very apt name since it seemed like an almost endless trip.

McKenzie talked about his friends Sarah and Luke and told her some of the history of the town. How it had been named after Luke's grandfather, since it was him who first settled in the area. He promised to take her to their ranch one day. The thought excited Verity, as she really liked Sarah and was certain she would feel the same about Luke. She hadn't spent much time with him but assumed if his wife was friendly, he would be too.

"There are a few cabins scattered about the hills, but we rarely see the occupants in town. I do check on them regularly, though." He pointed to one such cabin in the distance. "It's far too isolated for my liking, but they seem to enjoy living out here."

Verity was certain she wouldn't like it, and a shiver went through her at the thought. "It's not to my liking," she said quietly. "What if you were sick or injured? Do they live alone?"

"There are a couple of older ladies out this way. Widows. I've tried to get them to move into town, but they won't have it. The best I can do for them is check in and make sure they're all right."

She understood them, not wanting to leave. Having been uprooted from her own home, Verity could totally relate. It wasn't easy to do, and it left a feeling of dread in the pit of your stomach. "You're very kind, McKenzie. Not everyone would do that." It was true. Many people would simply leave those widows to their own devices and never give them another thought.

She reached across and placed a hand on his knee. McKenzie stared at her hand as though it had burned through to his skin. Suddenly, he reached out and placed his hand over hers. Without warning, he lifted her hand to his lips and kissed it. Warmth spread through her, and a smile came to her lips.

It wasn't long before the buggy slowed, and they pulled into a clearing off the side of the road. "I thought you might like to go for a bit of a stroll. There's a stream not far from here. Pure water that's good enough to drink." He pulled on the brake and climbed down off the buggy, then helped Verity down too. As he lifted her, he stared into her eyes, and Verity was mesmerized. He was so handsome, this husband of hers, and she got lost in his eyes every time she stared into them. When she'd had no choice but to become a mail order bride, she had no idea she would fall in love with her husband.

Oh, she knew very well she couldn't fall in love with him so quickly, but she did have strong feelings for him. More likely than not, she was falling for his kindness and his caring ways. She barely knew the man, although each time she learned something new about him, she liked him even more.

McKenzie slowly lifted her to the ground, then put his arms around her. Verity leaned her head against his chest and listened to his steady heartbeat. Her arms slipped up around his waist, and she let herself mold into him. She glanced up into his face, and McKenzie leaned down to her, then kissed her gently. It was such a chaste kiss, and she wanted more. She felt so comfortable, wanted, and protected with this man and never wanted him to let her go.

"We need to stop if you want to see anything," he said with a chuckle in his voice. "I'll gladly stay like this all day, but…" he paused. "It's probably not a good idea." His hand came up and caressed her cheek, and a shiver went down her spine.

She took a step backward. He was right on both counts. She could stand like that all day, but it would be a wasted trip if they stayed where they were. A walk would get the kinks out from sitting in the buggy for so long. "I agree. We should go." She pulled her coat up around herself and began to walk into the woods.

"Verity." She stopped and turned to face him. "Wait for me. It can be dangerous in there." He hooked his arm through hers, and they headed toward the stream. She didn't care where she went, provided McKenzie was right there by her side.

Chapter Six

Two Weeks Later…

McKenzie stood aside and watched as a number of passengers left the stagecoach, as he had done every day for the past two weeks. Most were locals, but two were total strangers. He waited while the stagecoach driver removed their luggage and deposited it next to them.

He observed unnoticed as the young woman was collected by a local rancher, then the pair headed to the church. He knew from personal experience the woman would be a mail order bride. It made him smile.

The lone man, however, was another story. As he leaned down to collect his luggage, McKenzie noticed the gun that was holstered against his chest and approached the stranger. "Excuse me, Sir."

The newcomer glanced up, his eyes glued to the sheriff's badge on McKenzie's chest. He straightened up to his full height and studied the man standing in front of him. "Can I help you, Sheriff?"

If he thought he was going to intimidate McKenzie, he would be sorely disappointed. "Can we have a chat? My office, if you don't mind." The man grimaced. "It's more private there."

"Of course."

"I'll take care of your luggage," the driver said, then moved it into the coach office where it would be safe.

They moved off, and McKenzie introduced himself. "Sheriff McKenzie Dunn. We're just over here." He indicated the Sheriff's Office down the street. "What are you, a bounty hunter or investigator?"

The man extended his hand. "Sam Hatchett, bounty hunter."

"Bounty hunter, eh? Don't get many of those out this way."

Hatchett pushed his well-worn hat further back on his head. "Don't suppose you do. What gave me away?" This time, he scratched his head.

"Your gun. Next time maybe keep your coat buttoned up." The two entered the small office, and

McKenzie offered the man a seat. He indicated the *Wanted* posters peppering his wall. "Which of these are you after?" He had a bad feeling about this but kept his thoughts to himself.

He studied them momentarily, then looked away. "None of those. I'm looking for a woman, as it happens."

"A woman?" His heart thudded. This was the moment he'd been dreading.

"She stole a considerable amount of expensive jewelry. There's a large reward for bringing her in *with* the stolen items."

McKenzie was immediately on alert. The woman had to be his wife, and the jewelry...well, he knew all about that too. Louis didn't muck about sending someone to do his dirty work. Fury built up inside of him, but outwardly he kept his cool. "Is that so?" he drawled, not giving anything away.

"The reward from this job will mean I can retire from this sort of work once and for all. This is a mug's job – a man can't keep doing this sort of work forever."

It took all his effort not to flinch at his words. A prize that size meant Hatchett had a vested interest, especially knowing he could retire on the reward. There was no doubt in McKenzie's mind he would be like a dog with a bone.

Trying to take his attention away from this unwelcome information, he glanced past Hatchett's shoulder and out onto the street. He inwardly flinched as his pretty wife strolled along the boardwalk and into the diner. He was relieved when she was inside and out of sight.

"Don't suppose you can. A bit like a Sheriff. I don't see myself sitting here in twenty years' time. Even ten years will be too much." He rubbed his hand across his chin. "It's a hard life, but I suspect being a bounty hunter is far harder."

"You got that right."

McKenzie wanted to keep him talking and away from the streets and his wife. "I suppose you do have a license?" He extended his hand, waiting to see the license he had no doubt existed.

Hatchett's eyes opened wide in surprise. "You don't believe me?"

McKenzie rubbed a hand across his unshaven chin again. "A man can't be too careful these days. People pretend to be all sorts of things."

Hatchett reached into his wallet and pulled out his bounty hunter license. It was old and in a state of disrepair. It was almost falling to pieces. There was no doubt this man was who he said he was, but keeping him away from Verity could prove to be difficult.

He checked the paper over, being as careful as he could not to destroy the license. "This is almost expired." He spied the date – only a month left on it.

"I'm hoping to find the jewelry thief before then and not need to renew." He reached out his hand in a silent demand for his license to be returned.

McKenzie had no valid reason to keep the man any longer. "Well, thank you for coming in and explaining yourself. I would prefer you don't wear that firearm." He indicated the gun on the bounty hunter's chest. "This is a peaceful town."

"I have every right to wear it and use it if necessary," he said, his eyes piercing the sheriff's.

"Indeed, you do, but it would have to be extenuating circumstances, or I would be locking you up in one of these cells behind me." His words earned McKenzie a dark look.

Hatchett stood. "Thank you for your insights, Sheriff. Now I need to collect my luggage and book into the saloon."

Before McKenzie could say another word, the dreaded bounty hunter was gone.

The moment Hatchett was out of sight, McKenzie hurried over to the diner. No doubt the bounty hunter would have a description, if not a photograph of Verity. Although, if he did have an image of her, why didn't he show it to McKenzie.

No doubt the man had no clear idea Verity was here because if he did, he surely knew she was his wife. That would have come up in their conversation, and yet, it didn't. Perhaps he was going from town to town, trying to sniff out a lead.

Focused on keeping his wife safe, McKenzie glanced about, ensuring the newcomer wasn't in sight. Gazing through the diner window, he noticed Verity through the open kitchen doorway. That would never do; at the very least, she needed to move further into the room and out of sight. He would be far happier if he escorted her home, and she stayed there, but he already knew what her response would be.

He opened the diner door and hurried inside. She glanced up and saw him standing there, and her face broke into a smile. His heart fluttered, and his entire being filled with warmth. When had he become so enamored with this sweet lady? He'd gone from not wanting her at all to being protective, and now he knew he couldn't live without her.

She began to scurry toward him. "No!" He almost shouted, and she cowered. McKenzie ran toward her. "Get back into the kitchen. Quickly."

The look on her face told him she'd guessed the truth. "My uncle is here, isn't he?" Her shoulders sank, and her hands were shaking. All color had drained from her face.

He took her in his arms and shook his head. "Not your uncle. He's put a bounty on your head. A bounty hunter has arrived in town." Both women gasped at the same time.

"Oh my Lord," Jeannie said, her voice shaking.

"You stay here for now, but out of sight. Keep away from the doorway, and don't leave until I return. I'm going to see Henry. Hopefully, he has some information by now."

Verity plopped down into a nearby chair.

He didn't wait for a response but left without another thought.

Henry was reading through a number of papers scattered across his large desk. He glanced up as McKenzie entered his office. "McKenzie. Just the man I wanted to see. Where is that lovely wife of yours? I have news."

McKenzie's heart thudded. "Good news, I hope. I don't think I can cope with any more bad news today." He pulled his hat off his head and sat down. Henry stared at him. "A bounty hunter has arrived in Carson's Hollow." He swallowed back the emotion that was threatening his very being. He couldn't lose Verity; couldn't bear it.

Henry picked up a letter and waved it through the air. "I have a copy of the mother's will, and your wife's ownership has been verified." He handed the letter over to McKenzie to see for himself. "I also have a letter from the jewelry shop that supplied all the items her father gifted to her. That has also been verified."

McKenzie sighed with relief. "What about her father's will?" He didn't care about her money if it was truly hers, but he didn't take kindly to people who swindled others out of what was rightfully theirs.

"That is going to take far longer. The uncle used *his* wealth to have the will sealed. I have applied to the courts to have it unsealed. It could take weeks or even months, but I'll continue to fight it. There has to be a reason he's done that."

McKenzie mulled it all over in his mind. "Let's see if I have this right – all of the jewelry belongs to Verity by law. But the uncle has locked the will." He rubbed a hand along his chin. "What do I do about the bounty hunter? I'm worried for my wife's safety."

Henry carefully added the letter to a folder marked *Verity Dunn*, and carefully filed it away. "Bring him here. I will explain the situation and send him on his way."

"There is no doubt in my mind that Louis will send more unsuspecting bounty hunters."

"Under false pretenses." Henry seemed lost in thought. "I suggest we leave the jewelry locked up here. That will keep it safe. You should look into having it stored somewhere safe anyway – either here or at the bank. It's worth far too much to keep at home."

McKenzie's eyes opened wide in surprise. "How much are we talking?"

"Are you certain you want to know?" McKenzie wasn't sure but nodded anyway. "The jewelry store receipts alone total over three thousand dollars."

McKenzie whistled, then gripped the edge of the desk. "You're right," he said with a shaky voice. "Please keep it locked up here. Work out your fee for doing so, and I'll fix you up."

Henry waved his hand in the air. "No charge. I want to know it's safe too."

McKenzie stood and had to hold the desk for support before he could leave. "Thanks, Henry. I'll go and find Sam Hatchett, the bounty hunter, and bring him back."

He donned his hat and left to find the dreaded bounty hunter.

"You know I won't be the only one chasing this bounty? Louis LeFebvre spread the word far and wide. And the reward for finding his stolen jewelry is substantial; two hundred dollars would have been the final payment on my ranch back home."

McKenzie's legs felt as though they would collapse under him. He should have realized a man like that would want to ensure his goal was met. *How could he do that to his niece?* His only remaining family, according to Verity.

"You do realize he probably wouldn't have paid out the reward, even if you delivered? That's the sort of person we're dealing with here." Henry was right. The man was evil, greedy, and had no scruples; it made sense that he would likely renege on his word.

"This town will be swarming with bounty hunters and private detectives soon. Mark my word." Hatchett stood. "I'm sorry to have caused you and your wife so much grief." He shook hands with McKenzie and then Henry. "I might as well leave town. There's no reason for me to stay now."

It got McKenzie to thinking. "If you have some time, I might have an idea to make it worthwhile for you to stay awhile." The two men strolled out of the solicitor's office and headed toward the diner.

McKenzie sat sipping coffee as he chatted to Sam Hatchett. For a bounty hunter, the man seemed to have high morals, which he found comforting. Of course, it could all be for show, but McKenzie didn't think so. He'd been a sheriff for more years than he cared to remember and was a good judge of character.

Verity placed two blueberry muffins in front of them and refilled their mugs. He reached out and held her hand as she turned to walk away. "Sam has agreed to be your bodyguard until the danger is over."

Her head shot up as he knew it would. Verity glared at her husband but didn't say a word. She then turned to the stranger sitting opposite her husband. "Thank you for the offer, but I don't require a bodyguard." She pulled her hand out of McKenzie's grip and quickly returned to the kitchen.

McKenzie turned in time to see the two women huddled together at the back of the store. It made him wonder what they were up to. They were planning something. He was certain and didn't trust either of them to do what he'd asked. He simply wanted to keep his wife safe, and to that end, he needed her to stay out of sight.

"You do understand that without your wife's co-operation this will be difficult?" Hatchett took another gulp of his coffee, then reached for a muffin. "Did your wife make these? She's a good cook."

It was all McKenzie could do not to chuckle. If only the other man knew the truth about his wife's culinary skills. At least now, after weeks of instruction, her cooking was edible. Despite that, after taking a bite he had to agree. "They are rather good." She had mastered a few other delicacies, and her repertoire was growing, thanks to Jeannie. "You should try her apple pie. It's very tasty too."

He took a large gulp of coffee, then continued. "I've telegraphed for at least one marshal, if not two, to be sent to Carson's Hollow. Unfortunately, even if they left today, they will still be some days arriving. In the meantime, we are the only wall of defense."

"Then we don't have a choice," Sam said. "It definitely helps that I know most of the bounty hunters in Montana. But a reward that big, they could easily travel from out of state."

McKenzie was becoming frustrated. This entire situation was turning into a debacle. Perhaps that's what Louis LeFebvre had planned. More people than McKenzie could hope to deal with himself, and one of them could snatch Verity out from under him while the others kept him busy. Only it wasn't going to happen. Sam Hatchett was a professional. He'd done this job for most of his adult life, and McKenzie was paying him well to look out for Verity. Now all he needed was for her to co-operate. "The next stagecoach is due tomorrow afternoon. Let's pray we are not inundated with new arrivals all at once." Sadly, he wasn't as confident as he sounded.

The sheriff suddenly stood. "I have to get back – as much as I want to, I can't stay here all day. I have rounds to do and paperwork to complete." He sighed, but it didn't make him feel any better. "Let me know if you need anything. You know where to find me."

He strolled into the kitchen and faced his wife. "I have to go now, but Sam will be here to take care of you." She screwed up her face, and if the situation wasn't so serious, it would have been laughable. But nothing about their current circumstance was funny, so he kept his thoughts to himself.

"I don't need…." Instead of letting her finish, McKenzie took her in his arms and kissed her – right there in the middle of the kitchen. He already knew what Verity would think about that, but he didn't much care right at this moment.

"I love you and want you to be safe," he whispered, so only his wife could hear.

She glanced up at him, surprise written all over her face. "I love you too," she said quietly. "But I had no idea you felt the same." She rested her head against his chest, and he couldn't help but caress her face.

It took all his effort to drag himself away, but he had little choice. He had to get back to work. At least he knew his wife was in good hands. What would happen tomorrow when the stagecoach arrived was another thing altogether. He hoped and prayed they would not come in droves. Even with two men to hold them back, it could turn into a fiasco beyond imagination.

Before he could change his mind, McKenzie hurried out of the diner and didn't look back.

Chapter Seven

McKenzie waited impatiently for the afternoon stagecoach to arrive. He had high hopes of no newcomers but knew it was wishful thinking. Sam was in the diner guarding his wife, despite him being the one who knew the bounty hunters.

It was a dilemma for sure – only McKenzie could send them packing, but only Hatchett knew what they looked like. In the end, he decided to go on gut instinct. When the stage finally arrived, he carefully scrutinized every person who alighted. He watched which ones were local, who was collected, and those who were totally alone. Everyone seemed legitimate. He would check again when tomorrow's stagecoach arrived and would continue to check daily until he was confident the danger was over.

When he was confident he hadn't missed anyone, he checked the stage driver's passenger list to be doubly sure. As he suspected, no one seemed out of place, so he headed to the diner, where he sat down opposite Sam Hatchett. "No one seemed amiss. As far as I could tell, everyone was who they appeared to be."

"Everything is fine here, too," Sam said right before he lifted the mug to his lips. "This is the easiest job I've ever had." His face broke out into a grin.

"Until it isn't." McKenzie pierced the other man with his eyes. "I wouldn't put anything past that man. He is evil and conniving and will do whatever it takes to get his hands on that jewelry. All he sees is money." The realization twisted in his gut. *How could he do such a thing to his niece?* It was beyond belief.

"When I met him, I had tremors running down my spine. I should have listened to my instincts. I knew something wasn't right."

"That's water under the bridge now. All that's important now is to keep my wife safe." He stared at Hatchett for a long moment. "I am trusting her life to you. Don't let me down."

"I won't, I promise you."

McKenzie glanced up as a mug of coffee was placed in front of him. Verity stood next to him, a strange expression on her face. *How much of the conversation did she hear?* He could have kicked himself – he should have been far more discreet.

She leaned in and kissed his cheek, then hurried away. She was back soon after, with a large piece of apple pie for each man, with clotted cream on the side.

"This looks delicious. Thank you." McKenzie looked up, and Verity put on a forced smile. As much as she pretended she was fine, he could tell how very stressed she was. He was glad she had the diner and Jeannie to turn to at a time like this. It would be far worse if she sat at home with nothing much to do. At least here, she was kept busy most of the day. She seemed to really enjoy it, too. As an added bonus, McKenzie could see the diner from the Sheriff's Office, and he could get there quickly should the need arise. It made him feel somewhat better.

"What do you think the chances are of more bounty hunters arriving?" This time McKenzie kept his voice low, hoping Verity didn't overhear the conversation.

"Truthfully?" Sam pushed the pie around the bowl, then glanced up at McKenzie. "It's highly likely. A bounty that high will bring them here in droves. Don't count on them coming by stagecoach, though. Some will be far more discreet."

It was exactly what McKenzie worried about. At least with Sam here to identity fellow bounty hunters, he had a fighting chance to weed them out.

"I think I'm getting a headache," he said quietly, not wanting to voice how he really felt. "This is turning into a nightmare."

"Be that as it may, don't you worry. Your wife is safe with me. And that's a promise." Sam finally lifted the spoon to his mouth and devoured the last of his pie.

The sheriff finished off his pie and took a large gulp of coffee, finishing it off before he stood to leave.

Verity scurried toward him. "You're leaving?"

She looked sad, and it made him unhappy, too. He would prefer to spend every waking moment with her, but instead, he had to trust Sam Hatchett to keep his wife safe. He pulled her close and held her in his arms. "I have to go, but Sam will ensure you are well protected."

She glanced at Sam but didn't seem to have the same confidence her husband felt. There was no way in Hades that McKenzie would leave her with the man if he didn't trust him. He leaned in closer and whispered in her ear. "You are safe with Sam. I wouldn't leave you otherwise." He reached up and caressed her cheek. "I have to go." He reluctantly pulled away, and Verity stood staring after him.

It almost broke his heart.

As hard as it was, McKenzie went about his day as though nothing was amiss. He did his rounds of all the stores, rode to outlying ranches to ensure all was well there, and checked on some of the elders of Carson's Hollow. Many of them were too frail, and in some cases, too stubborn to move into town. He would feel far more comfortable if they moved into the lodging house in town. At least there, they would be well fed, they'd be safe, and have company. It was high on his agenda, but he couldn't force anyone.

Charlie Hanson was also on his list of those who needed to live in town – for their own safety. Yes, he would be closer to the saloon, but McKenzie was certain if the old man had company, he wouldn't be so quick to fill his belly with booze. He tied his horse up outside Charlie's property and headed inside. Before he could knock on the door, Charlie was standing in front of him, a frown on his face.

"Come to arrest me, Sheriff?" The frown turned into a smile, and McKenzie knew the old man was joking.

"Not this time. I was passing by and thought I'd drop in and see if there's anything you need." It wasn't quite true. Charlie's place was off the beaten path, but McKenzie took the time, anyway.

The old man sniffed. "If ya say so." He stared at the sheriff, and they both knew Charlie didn't believe a word he'd said.

McKenzie glanced about as he was led inside. Boards were beginning to fall from the walls, and it bothered him. Last time he'd dropped in, sunlight shone through the roof. He asked Charlie's workers to fix it, and they did. At least now, the rain couldn't filter through.

The rest of the house was not going to be so easy to repair. The old ranch house was literally falling down around the stubborn old fool. The best way to fix it was to pull it down and start over.

He already knew the response he would get to that – it was a suggestion he'd made previously. McKenzie knew the townsfolk would be on board and pitch in to help, but the old man called it charity and would have none of it.

Rattling some of the boards with his hands, they almost fell off. "Why don't you come into town to live? Peggy has a couple of empty rooms and would love to have you there."

Charlie sniffed again. "I don't need no charity." He turned his back on the sheriff, then spun around again, almost losing his balance. McKenzie was by his side in a flash.

"We both know it's not charity. Your men would keep working your ranch, which would continue to give you an income. Besides, Peggy doesn't charge much for a warm bed and three solid meals a day." He knew he was beating a dead horse, but

McKenzie continued to plead his case. "The only difference is you would live in town."

"Three meals a day, huh?" Charlie stared at him. Was he finally considering the offer? Suddenly, he shook his head. "Nah, I couldn't leave this place. I was born here, an' me missus died 'ere. Too many memories."

McKenzie scratched his head. *Stubborn old fool!* "If you don't do something soon, we'll be pulling you out from under the rubble. And then it will be too late."

The old man walked over to the window and stared out. "I would miss all this." He spread his arms wide, indicating his ranch and all the animals spread across the range. Charlie turned to face him again. It seemed he might be finally considering the possibility, but McKenzie wouldn't get his hopes up. "Anyways, I can't get any of my stuff there. The wagon fell to bits."

McKenzie glanced about. What 'stuff' was the old man talking about? Nothing here was salvageable, and it certainly wasn't worth carting into town. "You don't need to take anything except your clothes and personal items like photos. Peggy supplies everything else you would need."

"Harrumph."

McKenzie knew he had to tread carefully. This was the closest he'd ever gotten to getting the old man to concede he needed to move out of this dilapidated building and to a place of safety. He didn't want to push the issue and have him suddenly refuse. "Well, I'll leave it with you. What say I come back in a day or two for your decision?"

Charlie stared at him for what seemed forever. "Sure thing, Sheriff. If 'n you're out this way, that is."

McKenzie tipped his hat at the old man. As he closed the door, he spotted Bart, the old man's foreman. It was time to have a chat and see if Bart and the workers were up to running the place if he convinced Charlie to move into town.

McKenzie ducked his head around the entrance to the diner.

Sam lifted his arm in greeting. "All is well here," he called out. "No strangers about, and it's been quiet."

He heard muttering coming from the kitchen and tried to resist the urge to see his wife, but the pull was far too strong. Instead, he strode toward the sound. Verity glanced up and smiled. Her hands were covered in flour, and her face held remnants of her cooking endeavors. Warmth flooded him.

"What have you been making?" He couldn't resist and brushed the flour from her cheeks.

"Cherry Cobbler." She looked so proud, and it made his heart swell. She leaned in a little closer. "You can have some for dessert if you'd like." She leaned over and picked something up. Before he knew it, she'd popped a cherry in his mouth. It was sweet and delicious, just like his wife, and flavor exploded in his mouth.

He swallowed down the delicious fruit before answering. "I'm sure I would like," he whispered, and she grinned up at him.

"Sit down, and I'll bring you a mug of coffee." She pushed him out of the kitchen before he had a chance to protest. McKenzie glanced out of the diner window and frowned. Two strangers headed toward the livery, no doubt to leave their horses. They'd come a long way – there was no railway here or nearby, and the nearest town was a little over a hundred miles away.

"Sam."

He indicated the two riders, and Sam's expression changed. "I know them. Best we cut them off before they go running off their mouths." He glanced across to McKenzie. "Stafford Owens and Joe Rawlins. If it's a dead or alive bounty, dead is how they always arrive."

McKenzie spun around as he heard Verity gasp. He glared at Sam. "Nothing to stress about," he said, pulling her into his arms. "I will sort those two out. Sam, you stay here and look after Verity." He stormed off toward the livery, his heart pounding. He wasn't sure if it was because Sam had scared his wife or because of the two strangers in town.

As he approached the livery, he tried to size them up. From the little Sam had told him, they were a force to be reckoned with. "Afternoon gentlemen," he said, then put his arms up in front of himself as two rifles were suddenly pointed at him. "Sheriff McKenzie Dunn. Mind putting them firearms down?" The rifles slowly went down, and McKenzie felt relieved. "We need to have a chat back at my office."

"You askin' or tellin'?"

"That would be telling. Follow me." Once inside, he turned to the two men sitting in front of him. "Which one is Rawlins, and which is Owens?" The men stared at each other, presumably wondering how he knew their names.

"I'm Stafford Owens," the shorter of the two men said. They were both rough looking, their hair down below their shoulders. Their clothes were ruffled and dirty, and each man needed a bath and a shave. Much like most of the bounty hunters he'd come across.

"And I'm Joe Rawlins."

"What is your business in Carson's Hollow?" Direct and to the point – he wasn't going to beat around the bush.

Again, the two men glanced at each other. "We're chasing a bounty," Rawlins said.

"Name the bounty." He watched as they stiffened.

"We don't have to do that."

McKenzie eyed them both, going from one man to the other. "In my town, you do," he said carefully. "Especially when I believe it's an illegal bounty."

Both men suddenly stood, and McKenzie did the same. "Sit down. I'm not through." They hesitated. "I have two empty cells back there, and as much as Jeannie's cooking is good, I doubt you want to spend the next few days here."

They reluctantly sat, each looking sideways at the other. "You're looking for a woman, am I right?" They sat without speaking. "Verity LeFebvre."

Joe Rawlins' head shot up. "How did you...."

"Verity is my wife."

Neither man said a word. "The bounty on her head is illegal. Louis LeFebvre has lied to steal what rightly belongs to Verity."

Stafford Owens glared at him. "You're just sayin' that 'cause she's your missus."

McKenzie felt the fury rise through him. "I have the proof. In fact, I'll walk you over to the solicitor's office right now, and he can show it to you. Not that I have to do that, mind you." Neither man said a word. "Otherwise, those cells are still empty."

Owens stood, and Stafford followed. "Right then, show us this *proof*." Owens said the last word as though he didn't believe a word McKenzie had said. He was ready to lock the man up right now. His temper was getting the better of him, but he showed as much restraint as he could muster.

He opened the door and led them to Henry's office. "Henry, these men are bounty hunters. Come for Verity," he said. McKenzie hovered in the doorway, and the solicitor pulled out the file.

"I have the proof right here," he said and showed the papers to the two men, careful not to let them get close enough to take the letters or even rip them up. McKenzie was keeping a close watch on them too. With people like this, you never knew what they would do. "I'm sorry you traveled all this way, but you were sent here under false pretenses."

"That's that then," Stafford said as he stood. "No hard feelin's, Sheriff."

But McKenzie trusted neither of them and would keep a close eye on the two. "How long are you here," he asked as they left Henry's office.

Stafford shrugged. "Long enough to rest our horses, and then we'll move on."

"See that you do. This is a peaceful town – we don't want any trouble." He would not hesitate to lock them up, and the bounty hunters knew it.

"No trouble from us, Sheriff," Owens said. "We just do our jobs and move on."

For some reason, McKenzie didn't trust them, but he had no cause to hold them, so he had to accept their word. For now.

Four days passed, and the two bounty hunters left town without bother, but McKenzie had a feeling deep in his gut the trouble wasn't over. A dark cloud hung over his head, and he was certain trouble was brewing.

As he waited for the stagecoach to arrive, he was certain something was about to happen. None of it good. He stood back as the step was placed in front of the door, and two women alighted. "Mrs. Henley, Mrs. Creighton," he said as he tipped his hat. Their husbands were there to greet them. His gut twisted as three complete strangers stepped off the stage. Two of the men looked as though they would take no nonsense, but they looked as far away from bounty hunters as you could get. They eyed his sheriff's badge and stepped aside.

The third man was of great interest to McKenzie. He wore a suit made of the finest material, and his hat was the best money could buy, he was certain. Not the sort of attire you'd expect to find in a small town like Carson's Hollow. "Excuse me, Sir," McKenzie said the moment the man was off the stagecoach.

The stranger's head shot up, and he stared at McKenzie and then his badge. He planted a false smile on his face. "What can I do for you, Sheriff?" he asked in what McKenzie was sure was a French accent. His heart thudded. *Was this Louis LeFebvre?* He was almost certain it was.

He'd come to find his niece himself. The words pounded in his head.

"Sheriff McKenzie Dunn," he said carefully, trying not to make this personal. "Might I ask what your business is here?"

The man looked him up and down, defiance written all over his face. "No, you may not."

McKenzie stood back for a moment and took in the man's words. "In that case, Sir, you will accompany me to the Sheriff's Office, where we will discuss this further.

He stared at the sheriff, then glanced about. "Do you know who I am?" Did he think money would get him off the hook?

"I have a fair idea." McKenzie reached out and tried to guide Louis toward his office, but the man resisted. It was then the two strangers stepped in.

"Marshal's Mercer and Gawne." The man reached behind him and pulled out a set of handcuffs. "Louis LeFebvre, I am arresting you for falsifying legal documents." The Marshal nodded at McKenzie. They obviously knew far more than he did.

"What are you talking about," Verity's uncle shouted. "Get your filthy hands off me." But it did him no good.

"Lead the way, Sheriff Dunn." McKenzie was very happy to comply with the request.

Two days later…

McKenzie loaded up the buggy with Charlie's meagre belongings. He packed his clothes into a carpetbag and carried photographs of his wife against his chest. There was little else worth saving.

The furniture that had belonged to his grandfather and was well past being used would be burned. Everything else was either falling apart or not in a fit state to be used. Charlie's foreman, Bart, had promised to pull what was left of the building down and use it for firewood. It was in no state for anything else.

Charlie glanced back as they rounded the corner, a tear in his eye. "I'm going to miss the old place," he said quietly. "I've lived me whole life there."

McKenzie felt for the man. It would have been tough to leave like this, but it was time. The rickety old house should have been condemned years ago, but no one had the heart to do it. This way was far kinder.

"I just bet you're looking forward to your first meal at Peggy's." He glanced across at Charlie, who wiped a tear from his cheek. He was no doubt hoping he hadn't been seen. "The bed will be warm and comfortable too. Even better than the jailhouse." He smiled, but the old man was in no mood for talk, so McKenzie stopped talking until they arrived at Charlie's new home. There was no going back, and the old man knew that.

McKenzie helped him down from the buggy, then reached for his few belongings. Charlie clutched the photographs tightly and refused to let them go. It was understandable, so McKenzie let him have his way.

Peggy stood on the boardwalk, waiting to show Charlie his new home. "Welcome, Charlie. It's so nice to have you here." She walked inside with her new boarder right behind her. If it was the only win McKenzie had this month, he'd be happy. Hopefully, Charlie would be far too busy to visit the saloon.

Peggy introduced Charlie to the other boarders, although he would have known most of them already. "Coffee, Charlie?" she asked. "It's afternoon teatime. Sit down, and I'll bring you some cake." The old man's face lit up.

McKenzie slipped away quietly, pleased to see the old man's delight.

Epilogue

Twelve months later…

With his trial finally over, the fake Louis LeFebvre was jailed for multiple counts of fraud, including identity theft. Verity's real uncle had died some years ago, and this man, Claude Lavigne, had stolen his identity after somehow learning who Louis' brother was. He had waited patiently on the sidelines to carry out his devious plan. There was even some suggestion he may have killed Pierre, but there was no proof. Before her father's death was announced, Claude created a fake will, making him the sole recipient of her father's estate and everything in it.

Henry's investigation had opened the floodgates, effectively causing a chain reaction. The magistrate had become involved, demanding a copy of every

version of the will Pierre LeFebvre had ever made.
The fake will was the only one that couldn't be
verified. A check of the signature and those of the
so-called witnesses proved its lack of authenticity.
Apart from the fact that Pierre's solicitor did not
prepare this will. The real will had Verity inheriting
everything and was stored at the family's solicitor's
office.

Claude was jailed for fifteen years and would leave
jail a pauper.

That left Verity with ownership of her father's
entire estate, including the railway. All of which she
didn't particularly want. She was more than happy
living in Carson's Hollow with her handsome
sheriff-husband.

"Sign here and here," Henry told Verity. "Just to
clarify, you still have complete ownership of your
father's estate, but until you say otherwise, all
profits will go straight into your new charity
supporting women in need." Warmth filled her,
knowing no woman would ever have to live on the
streets or live in poverty. Not only would they have
somewhere safe to live, but they would be trained
in whatever vocation they chose. What a wonderful
legacy to her father. Indeed, both her parents.

"I didn't know him, but your father would be so
proud of you, Verity." Was McKenzie feeling as
emotional as she was at the decision she'd made? It

would help countless women, and in some cases, their children as well. "The renovations you ordered means over two dozen women can be housed at once."

"Not to mention the jobs your charity has created," Henry added.

Verity forced back the tears that threatened to fall. McKenzie was right – Father would be proud. He would be distraught at his brother's undiscovered death and the abhorrent and unlawful actions of Claude Lavigne. Not to mention angry at the way he'd treated her.

"None of it would have happened without your help," Verity said and meant every word. "All that's left now is to decide what to do about the jewelry. It is totally inappropriate to wear in Carson's Hollow." It broke her heart to give it away as it was the last piece of her parents that Verity had, but what choice did she have? It had been locked away in Henry's safe for over a year already.

Henry looked thoughtful, and she wondered what was going through his mind. He tapped his temple. "What if…" He thought for a moment, then shook his head. "No, that won't work, but I do have another idea."

Verity leaned closer, and she felt McKenzie move in, too. "You could *lend* it to the Ontario Museum. As you're aware, your mother's jewelry had been passed down through the generations. I'm certain they would be interested in displaying it, and it would be kept safe." Emotion flooded her. What an absolutely wonderful idea. "The jewelry your father gifted you would also be of interest, I'm certain." He winked. "We'll make it a package deal, and they won't refuse."

Verity sighed in relief. It was the perfect solution and one she could live with. She turned as she heard eight month old Pierre crying in his father's arms. "He has been so patient," she said as she began to stand, her hands on her swollen belly. "He is probably hungry."

McKenzie reached out to help her, and warmth flooded her. "He's wet too," he said, a grimace on his face. Despite all the angst and the dishonesty she'd endured, the best thing that had ever happened to Verity was marrying McKenzie.

She thanked God every day for His intervention in bringing her to Carson's Hollow.

The End

From the Author

Thank you so much for reading my book – I hope you enjoyed it.

I would greatly appreciate you leaving a review where you purchased, even if it is only a one-liner. It helps to have my books more visible on Amazon!

To read Sarah and Luke Carson's story, check out Sarah's Surrender, also by Cheryl Wright.

Enjoy Lawmen stories? Then you may enjoy these books of Cheryl's:

Rescuing the Lawman

The Widower's Christmas Wish

Eleanor's Dilemma

Contemporary Romance:

River Valley Lawmen Series

The Sheriff's Sweetheart

About the
Author

Multi-published, award-winning and bestselling author, Cheryl Wright, former secretary, debt collector, account manager, writing coach, and shopping tour hostess, loves reading.

She writes both historical and contemporary western romance, as well as romantic suspense.

She lives in Melbourne, Australia, and is married with two adult children and has six grandchildren. When she's not writing, she can be found in her craft room making greeting cards.

Check out Cheryl's website for a full list of her other books.

Links:

Website: *http://www.cheryl-wright.com/*

Blog: *http://romance-authors.com/*

Facebook Reader Group:
*https://www.facebook.com/groups/cherylwrightaut
hor/*

Join My Newsletter:

https://cheryl-wright.com/newsletter/

CPSIA information can be obtained
at www.ICGtesting.com
Printed in the USA
LVHW101525140821
695324LV00007B/17

9 780975 672938